SKYLANDERS SPYRO'S ADVENTURE

BATTLE FOR SKYLANDS

Grosset & Dunlap
An Imprint of Penguin Group (USA) Inc.

ISBN 978-0-448-46183-0

10 9 8 7 6 5 4 3

ALWAYS LEARNING   PEARSON

COULD YOU BE A
SKYLANDER?

DO YOU HAVE WHAT IT TAKES TO BE A SKYLANDS CHAMPION? OR, LIKE HUGO, WOULD YOU BE BETTER OFF LEAVING THE HEROICS TO OTHERS? FIND OUT BY TAKING OUR TEST—AND HOPE YOU DON'T TURN OUT TO BE A FOLLOWER OF THE DARKNESS!

1

A TROLL ARMY IS RAMPAGING THROUGH THE LAND, RAISING EVERY VILLAGE TO THE GROUND. WHAT DO YOU DO?

a) Spring into action, taking on every troll single-handedly and sending them running for the hills.

b) Gulp and hide in the bushes. Someone else will come and save the day after all, won't they?

c) Cheer them on! The villagers are doomed—DOOOOOOMED, I tell you!

2

WHAT'S YOUR IDEA OF A NICE, RELAXING DAY?

a) Saving the world three times before breakfast. And then doing it again before lunch and dinner!

b) Sorting the Ancient Skylands History section of the library into alphabetical order.

c) Enslaving the entire universe! *Bwa-ha-ha-haaaaaa!*

3

WHICH WORD BEST DESCRIBES PORTAL MASTER EON?

a) Awesome!
b) Magnificent!
c) Eon? That pathetic old loser? He shall bow before the Darkness!

4

WHAT WOULD YOU DO IF YOU HAD A PORTAL OF YOUR OWN?

a) Go on amazing adventures!
b) Pop into town and buy a brand-new bookmark.
c) Unleash the Darkness throughout the cosmos!

5. WHEN YOU GROW UP, WHAT WOULD YOU LIKE TO BE?
a) Brave and courageous!
b) Left alone to look at my books.
c) All-powerful!

6. WHAT DO YOU THINK WHEN YOU SEE THE CORE OF LIGHT?
a) I must protect it at all costs!
b) It could use a polish. Where's my duster?
c) Destroy it! Destroy it! DEEEESTROY IT!

7. WHAT'S YOUR FAVORITE COLOR?
a) Red! It's exciting!
b) Beige! It's boring and safe!
c) Color? COLOR? There will be no color when Darkness rules the land!

8. THE MABU MAYOR NEEDS YOUR HELP. ROCK WALKERS ARE STOMPING ALL OVER THE PLACE. WHAT DO YOU DO?
a) Swoop in and reduce them to rubble.
b) Pass the message on to Gill Grunt or Trigger Happy. It was probably meant for them after all.
c) Give them a helping hand by unleashing the Giant Clod-Hopping Hordes of DOOM!

9. WHAT DO YOU THINK OF CYCLOPSES?
a) Horrible, smelly servants of Darkness! Bash 'em into next week!
b) Shouldn't that be Cyclopsi? Hang on, I'll look it up.
c) Loyal, faithful servants of Darkness!

10. SPYRO IS . . .
a) Cool!
b) Braver than me.
c) My biggest enemy! Boo! Hiss!

VERDICT!

Mostly As: Yes, you've got what it takes to be a Skylander, or even a Portal Master as great as Eon himself!

Mostly Bs: You are a person after Hugo's heart. You just don't see the point in putting yourself in danger's way.

Mostly Cs: Oh no! You're a follower of Darkness! In fact, are you sure that you're not Kaos in disguise?

WHICH ELEMENT ARE YOU?

THE CORE OF LIGHT WAS CREATED FROM EIGHT ELEMENTS. THE SAME ELEMENTS GIVE SKYLANDERS THEIR POWERS TODAY. ANSWER THESE DEEPLY PERSONAL QUESTIONS AND USE THE STICKERS AT THE BACK OF THE BOOK TO DISCOVER WHICH ELEMENT YOU'RE MOST LIKE!

START
Which word best describes you?

TOUGH → Are you noisy or quiet?

REALLY LOUD! → Do you like pies?

NO

THE STRONG, SILENT TYPE

ACTION-PACKED

YES → What do you like to do at the beach?

PLAY IN THE SAND

BRAVE → What kind of movies do you prefer?

FUNNY → What do you like to do at the beach?

SWIM IN THE SEA

COLLECT SHELLS

SMART → Which subject do you prefer at school?

GYM

SPOOKY

NO

SCIENCE → Do you like playing tricks on people?

YES

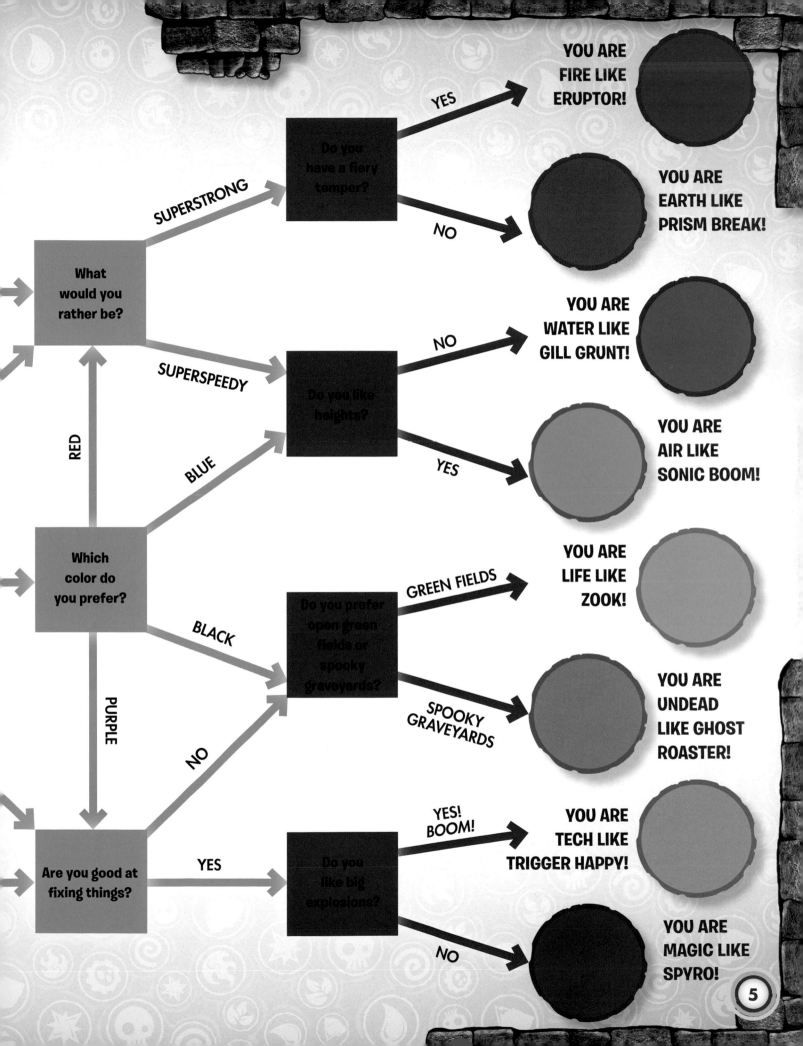

What would you rather be?

- SUPERSTRONG → **Do you have a fiery temper?**
  - YES → YOU ARE FIRE LIKE ERUPTOR!
  - NO → YOU ARE EARTH LIKE PRISM BREAK!

Which color do you prefer?

- RED → What would you rather be?
- BLUE → **Do you like heights?**
  - NO → YOU ARE WATER LIKE GILL GRUNT!
  - YES → YOU ARE AIR LIKE SONIC BOOM!
- BLACK → **Do you prefer open green fields or spooky graveyards?**
  - GREEN FIELDS → YOU ARE LIFE LIKE ZOOK!
  - SPOOKY GRAVEYARDS → YOU ARE UNDEAD LIKE GHOST ROASTER!
- PURPLE → Are you good at fixing things?

Are you good at fixing things?

- YES → **Do you like big explosions?**
  - YES! BOOM! → YOU ARE TECH LIKE TRIGGER HAPPY!
  - NO → YOU ARE MAGIC LIKE SPYRO!
- NO → Do you prefer open green fields or spooky graveyards?

WICKED WILDLIFE GUIDE

SKYLANDS PUTS THE WILD INTO WILDLIFE! WATCH OUT FOR THESE BEASTS, BUGS, AND BOGEYMEN!

CORN HORNET

Notable Features: Yellow and black stripes, evil-looking sting.
Habitat: The leafy glades of the Tree of Life.
Fact: Cyclopses love eating corn hornet maggots—especially on toast!
Survival Tip: A sting from one of these buzzing bullies is soothed by applying banana-flavored gravy to the affected area.

ROCKET IMP

Notable Features: Yellow skin, horns, pointed ears.
Habitat: Troll weapon factories.
Fact: This imp can store explosives in its own body. You don't want to know where!
Survival Tip: Rocket Imps can't see anything colored came-brown, so paint yourself from head to toe in the color!

GARGANTULA

Notable Features: Six hairy legs, beady red eyes, dagger-like fangs.
Habitat: Anywhere dark and spooky.
Fact: Hugo once found a gargantula in his bath. He didn't dare wash for a year afterward.
Survival Tip: Be warned—if you defeat a gargantula, swarmer spiders burst out of its body. Argh!

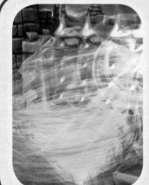

WINDBAG DJINNI

Notable Features: White, fluffy body, ugly face.
Habitat: Mountain tops, cloud kingdoms, and anywhere else high up.
Fact: Windbag djinnis smell like stale cotton candy.
Survival Tip: Windbags can blow you for miles. Grab on to something heavy . . . like a passing elephant!

FLAME IMP

Notable Features: Wide toothy mouth, long tail on head.
Habitat: Anywhere hot and steamy.
Fact: Flame Imps are the stupidest of the imps. They sometimes try to eat their own feet and only stop because they burn the insides of their mouths.
Survival Tip: Get too close and you'll find yourself whipped by that red-hot tail!

STUMP DEMON

Notable Features: Terrifying stare, a bite worse than its bark.
Habitat: Haunted forests and creepy crypts.
Fact: Stump Demons can live for hundreds of thousands of millions of years (provided they watch their diet).
Survival Tip: The best way of surviving a Stump Demon attack is to avoid them in the first place.

SKULLS

HEX HAS UNLEASHED A STORM OF SKULLS. CAN YOU FIND SEVEN SKULLS THAT ARE DIFFERENT FROM THE REST? THE ANSWERS ARE ON PAGE 16.

DID YOU KNOW?

Many inhabitants of Skylands are wary of Hex and suspect that she has used her potent magical abilities for evil. Eon and her fellow Skylanders know differently—she is an ally to be trusted!

CHOMPIE CHASE

START

THE TREE OF LIFE HAS BEEN INFESTED BY CHOMPIES. CAN YOU HELP STEALTH ELF ESCAPE THE MAZE WITHOUT RUNNING STRAIGHT INTO THE PATH OF A CHOMPIE? THE ANSWER IS ON PAGE 16.

DID YOU KNOW?
WHEN A CHOMPIE BITES YOU, IT'S NOT BECAUSE IT WANTS TO EAT YOU. IT'S JUST SHOWING HOW MUCH IT CARES, APPARENTLY. AHHH, HOW SWEET!

EXIT

CRUSTY CODEBREAKER

HELP WHAM-SHELL DECODE THE SECRET MESSAGE. IT CONTAINS VITAL INFORMATION ABOUT KAOS! WHEN YOU'RE DONE, WHY NOT USE THE CODE TO SEND SECRET MESSAGES TO YOUR FELLOW PORTAL MASTERS? THE ANSWER IS ON PAGE 16.

A	B	C	D	E	F	G	H	I	J	K	L	M
18			14				7			13		

N	O	P	Q	R	S	T	U	V	W	X	Y	Z
22	15				20	11					1	

Line 1:
13 18 15 20 — 25 20 — 20 7 15 24 11 , 19 18 8 14 ,

Line 2:
18 22 14 — 25 22 6 24 17 14 25 19 8 1 — 20 3 17 8 8 1 .

Line 3:
7 17 — 10 18 22 11 20 — 11 15 — 11 18 13 17 — 15 16 17 24

17 !

Line 4:
20 13 1 8 18 22 14 20

TIPS

EACH OF THE BLANKS IN THE CODE HAS A NUMBER BENEATH IT. FILL IN THE LETTERS THAT CORRESPOND TO THE NUMBERS TO CRACK THE CODE. WE'VE STARTED IT FOR YOU.

Need some help cracking codes and cyphers? Here goes:

Look for single-letter words. They're probably "a" or "i."

How many times do individual numbers appear in the code? Count 'em. The most frequent is likely to be "e," the most common letter in the English language.

The most common three-letter words are THE, AND, FOR, WAS, and HIS.

SAY WHAT?

KAOS HAS CAST A SPELL THAT HAS MIXED UP THE SKYLANDERS' VOICES. USE THE STICKERS TO RECONNECT THE CHAMPIONS WITH THEIR OWN BATTLE CRIES. THE ANSWERS ARE ON PAGE 16.

"FEAR THE FISH!"

"SILENT BUT DEADLY!"

"ALL FIRED UP!"

"THE BEAM IS SUPREME!"

"ROCK AND ROLL!"

"BOOM SHOCK-A-LAKA!"

"FULL SCREAM AHEAD!"

"NO GOLD, NO GLORY!"

SPOT THE DIFFERENCES

A PORTAL MASTER MUST ALWAYS KEEP THEIR EYES OPEN. MISSING THE SMALLEST DETAIL CAN MAKE ALL THE DIFFERENCE IN A MISSION. TAKE THIS TEST TO SEE HOW OBSERVANT YOU REALLY ARE. THE ANSWER IS ON PAGE 16.

A   B   C   D

HERE'S WHAT TO DO

Look at the two pictures. Think they look the same? Think again! Eon has cast a spell so that there is a difference in every square but one. Can you work out which square is exactly the same in both pics?

GOOD LUCK!

A   B   C   D

Gill Grunt's
Pirate Attack Survival Guide!

Yo ho ho and a bottle of timbers!
Do you know what to do if pirates sail into view?
Gill Grunt is on hand to let you know!

Know the enemy—
and how to outwit them!

Captain Dreadbeard

The most villainous pirate ever to sail the 7,024 seas is Captain Dreadbeard. His only weakness is his love of card games. His favorites are Trouser Snap, Oscar's Boot, and Old Mermaid. If you beat him at a game, he's honor-bound to let you go.

Evil teeth!

Evil hook!

Evil shoes!

Supersharp cutlass!

Coarse hair!

Fearsome fangs!

Seadog Pirate

This canine chump thinks of nothing but loot! He spends his whole life searching for treasure only to bury it again. Weird! Your best chance is to quickly fake a treasure map and send him off on a wild goose chase.

Blasteneer

The worst thing about this scurvy wretch is that he constantly smells of wet dog. Oh, and his habit of carrying around a live cannon! Try stuffing sheep into the cannon's barrel while he's having his midday nap.

Massive cannon!

Squiddler

These menacing mollusks aren't just interested in treasure. They want to rule the oceans! Luckily, they are terrified of seafood cookbooks. Have one handy at all times, with the recipe for deep-fried squid bookmarked.

Googly eyes!

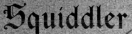

Mollusk mortar gun!

Did you know?
Pirates hold an annual sea shanty talent show—but it always ends in an argument, so no one has ever actually won.

Anchors ahoy!

Squidface Brute

The real muscle on a pirate ship! So strong he can use the pointy parts on an anchor like a pile-driving pickax! Best avoided, but if you can't, move quickly and hope that he gets his anchor stuck in the floor planks!

Cold, staring eyes!

Bulging muscles!

Message in a Bottle

Gill has discovered a secret about Captain Dreadbeard. Unscramble the tiles to reveal the message! The answer is on page 16.

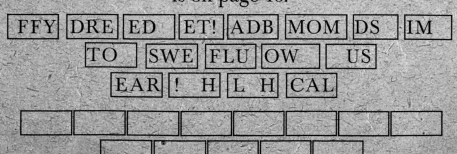

FFY	DRE	ED	ET!	ADB	MOM	DS	IM
TO	SWE	FLU	OW	US
EAR	!	H	L	H	CAL

The answer is on page 16.

SPEAK LIKE A PIRATE! ARRR!

Pirates are cruel, but they're also a bit dumb. If you learn to speak like them, you might be able to fool them into thinking you're a pirate, too! Here are a few key phrases:

AHOY!
Hello there!

ALL HANDS ON DECK!
Everyone needs to help!

AVAST!
Stop!

AVAST BEHIND!
My, what a large bottom!

AYE!
Yes!

AYE AYE!
Okay, okay. Don't go on about it!

BOOTY!
Treasure!

EVERYTHIN' SHIPSHAPE?
Is everything nice and clean?

LAND AHOY!
Look! There's some land!

LANDLUBBERS!
Anyone who doesn't like the sea!

SHIVER ME TIMBERS!
What a surprise!

YO HO HO!
How very funny!

ARRR!
I can't think of anything else to say, so I will make this noise instead!

TRUE OR FALSE

IT'S TIME TO TEST YOUR KNOWLEDGE OF SKYLANDS AND ITS CHAMPIONS, YOUNG PORTAL MASTER. BELOW ARE NINETEEN FASCINATING FACTS ABOUT OUR MAGICAL REALM. THE ONLY CATCH IS, SOME OF THEM AREN'T FACTS AT ALL. SO, WHICH ONES ARE TRUE AND WHICH ONES ARE NO-GOOD, FILTHY LIES? THE ANSWERS CAN BE FOUND ON THE NEXT PAGE.

1 Hugo has an irrational dislike of sheep. In fact, it borders on absolute terror. He thinks they're planning to take over the world. Baaa!
☐ TRUE ☐ FALSE

2 Gillmen are the best singers in all of Skylands.
☐ TRUE ☐ FALSE

3 A race known as the Benevolent Ancients first unleashed the Darkness.
☐ TRUE ☐ FALSE

4 Cyclopses are kind, sweet-smelling creatures.
☐ TRUE ☐ FALSE

5 If you've got enough gold, you can buy the right to be called Portal Master.
☐ TRUE ☐ FALSE

6 When Kaos destroyed the Core of Light, he turned Spyro and the Skylanders into tiny statues.
☐ TRUE ☐ FALSE

7 Portals of Power can also be used to travel through time.
☐ TRUE ☐ FALSE

8 The Arkeyans built the Core of Light.
☐ TRUE ☐ FALSE

9 Ghost Roaster's real name is Olav.
☐ TRUE
☐ FALSE

10 Flynn is irresistible to women.
☐ TRUE
☐ FALSE

11 Giants, despite their misleading name, are very, very small.
☐ TRUE ☐ FALSE

12 Trolls have a special day each year when they promise not to blow things up.
☐ TRUE ☐ FALSE

13 Lava Creatures like Eruptor are calm, controlled, and collected at all times.
☐ TRUE ☐ FALSE

14 Camo once caused a melon to explode all over Master Eon's alarmed face.
□ **TRUE**
□ **FALSE**

15 Kaos loves trees.
□ **TRUE**
□ **FALSE**

16 The Undead are scared of pies.
□ **TRUE** □ **FALSE**

17 Flameslinger's magic boots were a gift from an enchanted goblin.
□ **TRUE** □ **FALSE**

18 If Spyro spends too much time in the presence of dark magic, he becomes Dark Spyro.
□ **TRUE**
□ **FALSE**

19 Lightning Rod considers everyone else in Skylands to be "girlie"— especially girls.
□ **TRUE**
□ **FALSE**

ANSWERS

1. True. Even the sight of a woolly sweater is enough to make him need to rest.

2. False. Gillmen love to sing, but they sound like warthogs gargling pudding.

3. True. Their foolish experiments with magic first let the Darkness in.

4. False. They are mean, selfish, and smell worse than Kaos's old boots.

5. False. It's a talent you are born with. Which means that you are extremely lucky!

6. True. Not only that, but he banished them to Earth, too.

7. True—although no one has attempted time travel through a portal for centuries. Or so we believe.

8. False. It was the Benevolent Ancients trying to make amends for releasing it in the first place.

9. True. He was the finest chef in all of Skylands.

10. False. Just don't tell him!

11. False. They. Are. Giant!

12. True. You can tell when it's that day by their unhappy little faces.

13. False. You're kidding, right? They're liable to blow their tops at any moment.

14. True. But Eon didn't mind—and soon after, Camo became a Skylander.

15. False. He maintains a bizarre suspicion that they "are up to something."

16. False. They can't get enough of them!

17. False. He was actually given them by a fire spirit he rescued from drowning.

18. True. He uses dark magic to fight evil, but always runs the risk of being consumed by darkness.

19. True. And few are brave enough to argue with him!

ANSWERS

PAGE 7 STORM OF SKULLS

PAGE 8 CHOMPIE CHASE

START

EXIT

PAGE 9 CRUSTY CODEBREAKER

The secret message reads:
Kaos is short, bald, and incredibly smelly. He wants to take over Skylands!

PAGE 10 SAY WHAT?

GILL GRUNT
"FEAR THE FISH!"

STEALTH ELF
"SILENT BUT DEADLY!"

SPYRO
"ALL FIRED UP!"

BASH
"ROCK AND ROLL!"

PRISM BREAK
"THE BEAM IS SUPREME!"

DOUBLE TROUBLE
"BOOM SHOCK-A-LAKA!"

SONIC BOOM
"FULL SCREAM AHEAD!"

TRIGGER HAPPY
"NO GOLD, NO GLORY!"

PAGE 11 SPOT THE DIFFERENCES

The square that is exactly the same is 3C.

PAGE 13 MESSAGE IN A BOTTLE

The message reads:
Dreadbeard's mom used to call him Fluffy! How sweet!

EXTRA STICKERS